J
ICE

Ice Age collision course:
Welcome to Geotopia

03-16-17   CHILDREN:EASY READER

Welcome to Geotopia

SIZZLE
PRESS

A division of Bonnier Publishing
853 Broadway, New York, New York 10003
Ice Age: Collision Course TM & © 2016 Twentieth Century Fox
Film Corporation. All Rights Reserved.
SIZZLE PRESS is a trademark of Bonnier Publishing Group, and
associated colophon is a trademark of Bonnier Publishing Group.
Manufactured in the United States LAK0516
First Edition 10 9 8 7 6 5 4 3 2 1

ISBN 978-1-4998-0307-5 (pbk)
ISBN 978-1-4998-0308-2 (hc)

sizzlepressbooks.com
bonnierpublishing.com

ICE AGE COLLISION COURSE

Welcome to Geotopia

By Suzy Capozzi

SIZZLE PRESS

Hi. My name is Sid.
I am a smooth-talking sloth.
At least *I* think so.

These are some of my best buds.
Manny is a woolly mammoth.
Diego is a sabre-toothed tiger.
Buck is a weasel.
We make up a fun herd!

We always have
some wild adventures.
One time,
we saw a huge fireball
high in the sky.

It was a big rock called
an asteroid.
It was headed for Earth!

Buck loves adventure.
He also loves to help out.

He had an idea
where the asteroid would land.

We decided to go to the spot
Buck had plotted out.
We took our families
and a few friends, too.
We walked…

and walked.
And the asteroid got closer
and closer.

We made it to the spot!
The walls there shimmered
and shined.

"Welcome to Geotopia!"
said a pretty sloth
named Brooke.

Teddy greeted us, too.
He is super-strong.
He was so excited
to show us around Geotopia.

"We love having visitors!"
he shouted.

Geotopia is a huge geode.
A geode is a rock with
crystals inside.

Geotopia is so big that
all the Geotopian creatures
live inside it!

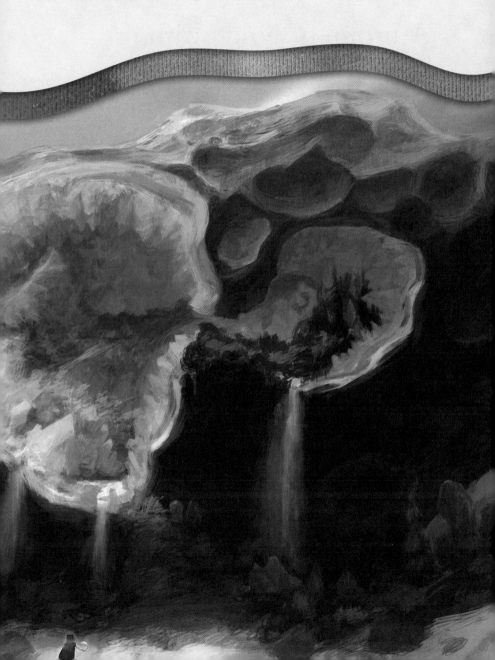

All those creatures
are kooky and colorful!
One was playing a guitar.
A group of wild animals
played chess.

And a big blue rhino
strutted around
with a crown of flowers.

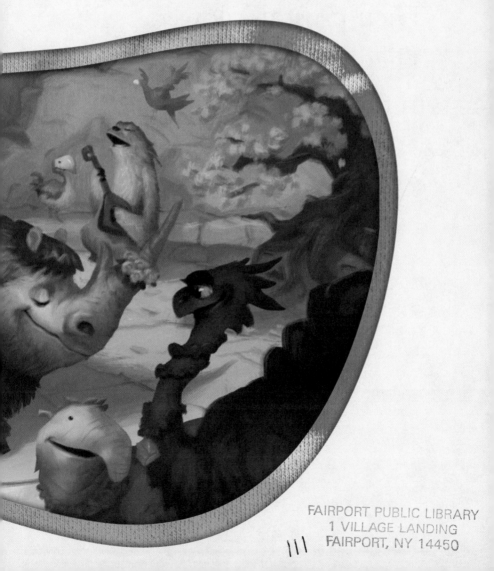

111

Other animals danced
and spun around.
They held crystals.
Their crystals glowed.
They threw flowers
in the air.

Wacky yaks and shovelmouths
swung from the vines.
And unicorns flew by.

They sure know how
to party
in Geotopia.

We spotted
a pair of petrals.

Next we met
some groovy aardvarks
and an ox.

Brooke and Teddy took us
down a crystal path.
Bong, bong, bong!
An animal hit a gong.
It got very quiet.
All eyes were on a furry bush
in the center.

"Here he is…the supreme
serene," said Brooke.
The bush started to move.
It wasn't a bush.
It was a llama doing yoga!
"Greetings, mammals,"
said the Shangri-Llama.

Buck tried to talk
about the meteor.
But the Shangri-Llama
paid no attention and did some
crazy yoga poses.

Luckily, the others
listened to Buck.
They saved the earth.
With the help of his
new friends, they stopped
the asteroid.
What a great day in Geotopia!